LOUISIANA LAGNIAPPE

BIG UNEASY 3.0

PAULINE BAIRD JONES

PBJ

ISBN: 978-1-942583-81-3

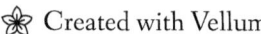 Created with Vellum

LOUISIANA LAGNIAPPE

ABOUT LOUISIANA LAGNIAPPE

A Reunion, a murder, and a wedding... What's next?

Becca Smith Poole should have known her fiftieth high school reunion would be anything but normal - especially when a dead body turns up! Renowned for her problem-solving skills, Becca is determined to discover who the murderer is - and if her former high school crush is still as handsome as he was in their younger days. The first will take some time to solve, the second one took her breath away.

Retired detective Zach Baker has been lonely since the last of his Baker's dozen moved out. When he sees Becca Smith's picture in the "where are they now" brochure, he wonders if this might be a first chance for him with the gal he could never connect with in high school. But before he can ask her out, a murder breaks up the party.

Lucky for him, his son's upcoming wedding is full of

problems requiring Becca's professional problem solving touch. Can a retired cop and a mystery reading problem solver unmask a killer before the wedding? Even more challenging, can Zach convince Becca that there is no end date for falling in love?

Dive into the next installment of the Big Uneasy series that reviewers have said will "make the reader feel as if they've been plopped down right in the middle of the Big Easy." Get Louisiana Lagniappe: The Big Uneasy 2.5 now!

PRELUDE

Fifty years.

It had been fifty years since Rebecca Smith Poole had graduated from high school.

Dang.

When Becca got the email from Lisa Linda Bailly, their senior class president, she'd had to do the math twice because it couldn't have been *that* long.

Only it had been that long. Every minute of that long.

So much for the class that was going to beat old, who would live forever. With very few (possibly chemical and/or medically induced) exceptions, they'd become gray hairs, or no hairs, the oldsters that back then they'd thought had one foot in the grave.

Anyone looking into the room would see a bunch of candidates for Senior Discount Day at just about anywhere. Lots of shoulders bent by gravity—not to mention other bits sagging from its evil grip. Here and there she caught glimpses of the young people they'd been in the septuagenarians they were now. They were here because fifty years ago they'd shared four years in the same high school, a lot of it spent in this gymnasium. It was kind of shocking that such a slender connection, that something that—with the hindsight of years—was so fleeting, had gathered their class's survivors in from all over the country.

In high school, they'd been divided into small clusters based on reasons that made no sense now. What would they even talk about, she'd wondered, as she'd hesitated over her RSVP. She was glad she'd come. They might have more in common now than they'd had back in high school.

They were all old.

They were the ones who weren't dead.

And they were more or less variations of the same shape.

Time had erased the other stuff, all the who-liked-who, and who-didn't-like-whom. The dividing lines had dissolved because what life they had left was too short. The theme of how freaking old they were was pretty much the go-to conversation that had started during the mixer—where they'd actually mixed—after a brief period of "do you remember?" The only other digression from the main theme of the night was those who had grandchildren to brag about.

Becca smiled as Mary Joanne who-used-to-be-Rivet shared a story on the theme of the night.

"I swear she was fifteen or something and she's putting the blood pressure cuff on my arm, and she says to me, she actually says to me," Mary Joanne switched to a high-pitched falsetto, "Isn't seventy the new sixty?"

"She did*n't*." Bettina Bailey would have gasped it in the old days, but now all she could manage was a distressed murmur.

"Oh yes, she did. And I told her, no, sugar, the new seventy is still the old seventy."

And some days, Becca thought, it was the new eighty.

"She's squeezing my arm and having to tuck the saggy bits in into a tube, and she says to me, well, you're only as old as you feel."

"I would have slapped her..." muttered Dot, who used to be Becca's best friend in the way back when. Her family had moved away about a week after graduation—it had felt like the end of the world at the time.

"...but who has energy for that?" Daisy Dixie finished.

They all chuckled because they were all out past our bedtimes.

As more oh-my-gosh-we're-old stories flowed past her, Becca pushed aside her paper plate. She'd eaten as much as she could of the catered meal—there was something to be said for those senior servings, even if the idea had annoyed her at first—and looked around. The gymnasium had seen as much wear as her class. The dispirited school hangings looked the same, though they must have changed them out once or twice. Behind the lackluster food smells lingered the scent of dirty shoes and perspiration, and mixed with the smells their class had brought it, all of it now being pushed around by a desultory and probably ancient air conditioner. She smiled at the sight of Georgy Guidry snoozing in his chair. Just like old times. His wife, Barbara Betty, had her back to him while she caught up with—well, Becca needed to get closer with her cheaters on to see the name tag.

The tags had been Becca's contribution to the effort. Lisa Linda had initially been a little annoyed at the font size Becca had chosen—it made the tags take up about half a chest—but everyone loved them and the high school pictures Becca had added below the names. Becca had needed the name tag to recognize Dot who had apparently recognized Becca without a problem. Or she had been more farsighted than Becca. Upon a closer look, the remains of the girl she'd been were still very much there. And her voice sounded the same, both plaintive and resigned as she somehow managed to cut Becca out of the herd so she could catch her up on the past fifty years in the Life of Dot.

Becca kept her smile in place, nodding occasionally as the big clock over Dot's shoulder tracked how far past her bedtime it was. When Dot paused to take a breath, Becca pushed her chair back.

Pale eyes blinked. "Are you leaving?" Her tone quivered as if she might cry.

Becca lifted her empty cup. "I need more punch." Her gaze did another sweep, but she knew he hadn't come, even though he'd RSVP'd an acceptance.

Her secret crush—one so secret she hadn't shared it with her best friend. Or her diary. If her heart could have kept it from her brain, it would have. She couldn't remember now why it had been imperative to hide it, but whatever the reason was, it still had her in its grip.

"I thought someone said Zach Baker was coming," Dot complained.

Becca may have twitched.

"I used to have the worst crush on him," Dot continued.

"All the girls had a crush on Zach," said Daisy Dixie from Dot's other side. "He didn't come to the last one either." She and Bettina sighed in unison. "I heard he's still a dish. And a widower."

"With *thirteen* kids," Bettina pointed out, with a slight shudder, though she added, "They must all be grown though?" She cast a languishing glance toward the entrance and sighed again. "Donna May says that Zach could give Harrison Ford a run for his money in the looks department."

As she moved away, Becca wondered, had all the girls Zach hadn't dated in high school been hoping for a reunion movie moment tonight? After fifty years? Becca examined her hopes critically. No, she was long past hoping for movie moments, but it would have been nice to see him. Still a dish, aye?

And then, as if her thoughts—or their talk—had summoned him, he appeared in the doorway. She gave him a critical once over. Yep. Still a dish who could give Harrison Ford a run for his money. And he had enough of "it" left to make her heart skip a beat. Maturity had somehow made his lined face handsome and his gray hair distinguished. She'd been a widow longer than she'd been married, but she could honestly say she hadn't thought about Zach, hadn't wondered "what might have been" until the reunion planning began. He'd married twice, lost both wives, and there were those thirteen kids, she reminded herself—like the others her information had been culled from the "where are they now" booklet that Lisa Linda had compiled. This was the moment she should be grateful for unanswered prayers. Women did not age as well as men, and she couldn't imagine the kind of damage thirteen kids would have done if she'd been on the delivering end. She did know the damage her three had done and that was plenty.

As he hesitated in the double doorway, she might have sighed. It would have been nice to have one of those, we-went-out-a-little, lost-love, might-have-been memories from high school. She'd mostly been invisible for the four years. Of the very few guys who'd paid her brief notice, two hadn't survived and the others, to her relief, had declined to come. She'd read where they were now, and it wasn't pretty.

When Zach's gaze started to scan her direction, Becca changed course. The punch bowl would take her toward Zach, who had been spotted and hailed with delight by his old friends—the gals and guys he'd actually shared high school memories with.

It wasn't because she was afraid to talk to him that she slipped between two tables without attracting the notice of the occupants. She just wanted to see the notable events of the past fifty years table. Lisa Linda, Mary Magdalene, and Donna May had gone to a lot of trouble to put it together.

Wow, seen this way, the years seemed even longer. While she'd been living her life wars and walks on the moon, all kinds of technology, and a new millennium had happened. With each step, each event she felt older, so she moved on to the memorial display. Because looking at who had died would make her feel younger. Not. But it was better than going back to the Life of Dot, Part Two.

Like the last display, this one was chronological, starting with Michael David Lorante, who had died a couple of weeks after graduation.

Forever young, she thought, staring at the dimly remembered face. She moved slowly down the line. The time gaps were big at first, then started to close as their class aged and the years racked up. At the end, she stopped, a frown forming between her brows. John James Normand and Larry Garry Olivier had both died within the last two weeks. That was sad. And odd.

She did a minor double take to check the dates. They died exactly a week apart. She took the small step to the last memorial picture and did more than a double take.

Georgy Guidry? Born nineteen fifty-three and died...today?

She glanced back at his slumped figure. It was just a bad joke, she assured herself, and Lisa Linda would not be happy about it. They were all supposed to be grownups now. Georgy might think it was funny...

"Becca?"

Becca stiffened. That sounded like Zach. How did she know how he sounded after all this time? She turned around. It was Zach. Zach Baker looking at her, apparently wanting to talk to her. Wow. He looked better up close, which was not fair since she knew she didn't. He smelled good, too. Nice for her—time had been kind to him. Not so nice for him, since time had been a meanie dancing all over her face. The gymnasium's A/C wasn't up to the job, and she wished she had a fan. Not that it could wave away the wrinkles and sags. She reminded herself how old she was and her lips curved up as her sense of humor returned.

"Hi, Zach. You're late."

It had to be her imagination that he seemed pleased to see her. Which was, she reminded herself, because they were classmates and they weren't dead. This made her glance at Georgy again, but her gaze refused to stay there. Not when Zach Baker was a few inches away from her *by choice*. All her dreams come true—fifty years too late.

He grinned, and her heart might have skipped. Because it was old and not quite up to the trip down memory lane.

"I saw the menu."

"Our budget gets smaller every reunion," she pointed out, without rancor. Mary Magdalene had been in charge of the food. For someone who'd grown up in New Orleans, her palate was not great. "As the class gets smaller."

He nodded as if she'd made a good point. His gaze moved briefly along the memorial row. "The attrition rate is for sure getting higher."

It didn't seem to worry him. It didn't worry her that much. She wouldn't open the door and invite Death in, but she knew now that no one got out of this life alive. Her smile turned wry.

"Weren't we the class that was going to live forever? How delusional was that?"

"Everyone is delusional in high school," Zach pointed out. "We all thought we were invincible." A hint of sad entered his gaze, which felt like headlights beamed on her face.

Becca knew how to hold a gaze. She had to in her business, but it was the first time she felt like, well, a girl. With a guy. Almost young again. Like they had been an item way back when and now they were having a moment.

And then, because fate was mean, over Zach's shoulder Becca saw Bubba Pascal approach Georgy and give him a shake.

"Wake up, dude, and join the party," he said it loud enough for the words to echo around the gym, causing conversations to break off as everyone turned to look.

Just in time to see Georgy slide sideways off the chair and face plant on the gymnasium floor.

* * *

Zach had known the really large number that this reunion was, but he had not shared that information with his kids, or anything about this reunion. None of their business, for sure not need-to-know, especially when he knew it would result in old-man jokes, nudges, and significant grins. He knew he was old, knew it better than any of them, better than any of them would—until they reached his age, which was no use to him now.

So it was ironic that three of his children had been first, second, and third responders to the scene.

Ingrid had arrived first, carrying in her EMT gear at a jog, the intent look an indication that she did not yet know her dad was here. She and her partner had not spent a lot of time working on Georgy. He had been cold when Zach checked for a pulse. Considering how warm the gym was—and the untouched state of his plate—he must have died soon after sitting down.

Since he'd died while not in his doctor's care, the Coroner's office had to make an appearance. That brought Hannah to the scene. She hadn't noticed Zach either as she bent over Georgy. Something about the death had troubled her, so she called for a detective.

Who just happened to be Alex and his partner—the same partner who was also Hannah's boyfriend. Zach tried not to scowl at Logan Ferris. He wasn't a bad guy, just didn't like him dating his daughter.

Last time Zach had talked to Alex, he was off the night shift. So that was old news, since he now appeared to be back on nights. If Zach hadn't been trying to keep his head down, he'd have asked his son who he'd pissed off this time. Alex's upcoming wedding had mellowed him some, just not enough, it seemed.

Three Bakers—four if he included himself, which he was sure his kids wouldn't—what were the odds of that? In New Orleans, they called it a "baking" when more than one of them responded to a scene and "well baked" for three or more.

His staying out of sight was helped by Becca who had somehow managed to calm Barbara Betty and then herd their class away from what was to become a crime scene. What was even more interesting, none of his classmates appeared to notice they were being herded. He watched her—he told himself—to see how she did it, but he might have forgotten that part because he liked looking at her.

When she quit herding, he arranged it so that he ended up next to her again. He hadn't read all of the "where are they now" summaries in the booklet that arrived with the reunion details, but he'd read Becca's.

She was the one who got away, so of course, he was curious. Well, maybe she hadn't gotten away so much as he hadn't figured out how to bridge his inexperience and her shyness before they separated for college. As the years had passed, he'd been too busy to worry about what hadn't happened, but when he saw her picture again? He might have wondered if a guy could get a second chance.

Her picture hadn't been faked, he noted, taking careful note so she wouldn't notice him checking her out. She looked good. She was almost his height, her gaze direct and kind. When she glanced away, he glanced at her high school picture, comparing then to now. The years sat lightly on her, but he could tell she hadn't fought the years, had let life do what it was going to do while she did what she had to do. Which was—well, he wasn't quite sure what she did. *Creative Solutions*, her business name, could mean anything.

"How did you do that?" Zach gestured toward his milling former classmates.

She wiggled her fingers and grinned. "Magic." He gave her a look so she added, "My son calls it my super power and said if I'd been born a few years later I'd have been an ambassador or possibly a general. But I didn't discover my," she hesitated, then said, "herding skills until I had kids, so I'm not sure I believe him." She looked thoughtful. "And I'm not sure herding is a skill an ambassador needs."

"A general might find it useful." He liked the way

she laughed and her clear, soft voice. He was sure her skills were about more than herding. Look how she'd calmed everyone down. They all kept stealing looks at Georgy, but the screaming had stopped and no one was crying. Not even his widow.

"What is it that you do?" he asked. He was, he admitted, more interested in keeping the conversation going than in knowing what she did. He'd tried dating twice now, and it had made him feel old. And tired. Becca didn't make him feel old. Or tired. Not that this was a date, but even an old guy could hope for more time with a might-have-been high school flame.

"I solve problems," she said, her smile exposed a lot of laugh lines around her mouth and eyes. "When my husband died, I needed something I could do and still be a parent. Something I could...control."

Zach knew why she hesitated at the word control. Kids and control didn't go together. He'd had to look for a second wife after Georgette died. When Helen died, too, well, it was a good thing Alex was old enough to help out because no woman wanted to take on a man with thirteen kids. He'd gotten used to being without a wife, but when his last daughter had graduated from law school and moved out, he realized he missed having a woman who wasn't his daughter around. Missed the way a wife changed the energy from house to home, the warmth he couldn't make happen. Plus his kids kept worrying about him, and they had made Laura move back in to take care of him. Having her in the house made him worry more about *her*. And Laura needed to be free of her old man, free to live her life, not his. He needed a wife, a companion who was his age. But the world had changed a lot since he'd wooed Helen—and not for the better.

If he'd done the math right, Becca had been alone at least as long as he had. If she had missed having a man around, she'd probably gotten over it, or she would have married again. He didn't think she was dating if her social media profile was right. And he was kinda proud he'd managed to check it without having to ask for help from any of his kids.

He'd felt a bit like a stalker checking her out ahead of the reunion—and he wouldn't have come if he hadn't known she'd be here—but most of the class who were online had friended each other when the reunion talk started. It hadn't been as bad as he'd expected, the friending crap. It felt okay to catch up with long lost classmates. Especially this one.

She'd fallen silent, which wouldn't have bothered him if he wasn't trying to work up the courage to ask her out.

"So what do you do?" He prompted when she stopped. He liked her eyes, liked the way the color in them changed as she talked. Liked that she wasn't young. She'd know about aching bones and a body that felt older on the outside than it did on the inside.

"My son calls it the mom thing, but without the guilt trip." She chuckled again. "I come in when a situation is too complicated, say during a wedding or big family events. I'm the neutral person when family is too...too invested. I smooth out the bumps or at least make them smaller. Sometimes I help with divorces—not legal advice—but just hand-holding and steering through the shoals. Other times, all I do is connect people with the person or business that can help them. I'm that one step removed, the longer view person who can find the compromise place. It's not perfect because people are still people, but well, I guess the short version is that I solve problems."

Creative Solutions. Creative solutions to problems. Zach straightened, his gaze finding Alex, who had just spotted his dad, based on the sudden stiffening of his son's shoulders and the sudden glare toward Zach. Alex, who was getting married to a gal tangled in complications. Family complications. And Family complications. He'd been kinda amused watching his first-born flail, but now the thought of helping him out was appealing. If Becca helped Nell and Alex, well, he could spend more time with Becca—the kind of time that closed the distance without all the pressure of dating.

He angled her direction, subtly separating her from the cluster of people near them. He inhaled the sweet scent of woman and flowers—damn, he'd missed that— and smiled down at her.

"So, how does someone go about hiring you?" Out of the corner of his eye, he saw Alex closing on them.

"You have a problem?" She sounded doubtful. Or maybe it was surprised.

"Well, my son has a problem." He nodded to indicate him. "He's getting married again."

Her gaze shifted to watch Alex with what he hoped was interest. "I see," she said.

She looked back at Zach, and he had a feeling she thought she saw the problem. She probably thought it was a second marriage problem. If only. No, Nell and Alex were snared in the mess of a cop, and the son of a cop, marrying a gal related to two mob families, not to mention one grandmother who might or might not get out on bail in time for the nuptials, and another that—well, he didn't know how to describe Nell's other grandmother, in or out of his brain. He must have let some of that show because her gaze narrowed. He smiled, hoping she couldn't see into his dark heart and mind. He might have been out of the game for more years than he cared to count, and Becca couldn't be more different than his late wives, but she did have one thing in common with them.

There was an elusive air about her, a wariness that required a careful approach. He needed to get her involved in him and his family before she realized what was happening.

Alex stopped in front of them, his gaze moving from Becca to his dad.

"Dad."

"Son, I'd like you to meet Rebecca Smith—"

"Poole," Becca finished.

"Right. This is my son, Alex."

"Ma'am." Alex's tone wasn't warm.

Rebecca held out her hand. "Call me Becca," she said with a smile.

After a long pause, Alex's shoulders relaxed. Zach wasn't sure his son realized it, but it made Zach hide a grin.

Oh yeah, she was good. He glanced at Becca and caught sight of her friend...Dot—that was her name wasn't it—over Becca's shoulder. She stared them with an odd look on her face. He met her gaze and arched a brow. With something that might have been a smile, she turned back to the group she was with and lifted her cup to her lips. Her gaze darted their way again, and when she saw Zach still looking, she shifted, so that her back was to them.

Zach half shrugged. She'd always been an odd one. Couldn't figure out how Dot and Becca had ever been friends.

"I'll need a statement from both of you," Alex said, with extreme reluctance. There was a bit of "we'll talk later" in there, too. Sometimes his kids forgot who was the parent and who wasn't.

"There's something you need to see," Becca said.

"Something?" Zach wasn't sure which one of them asked it first, the one-word question from them both so close together it sounded like an echo.

"On the memorial table. There's one for Georgy."

Alex made a sharp half turn toward the display, his brows shooting up. He and Becca followed Alex to the display. All three of them stared down at the framed picture.

"Today's date," Zach said slowly.

Alex rubbed his chin, then looked back where a bagged Georgy was being loaded onto a stretcher.

Becca gave Zach's arm a small nudge and when he looked at her nodded at the row of memorials.

"The last two," she murmured barely loud enough for his old ears.

Zach's brows lowered, then rose as he assimilated the dates. Two deaths in the two weeks before the reunion? He opened his mouth to point this out to his son, but Alex cut him off.

"You're retired, remember, dad?"

Zach felt his gaze narrow as it clashed with Alex's. Zach reached up like he was using a key to turn his brain off. His son's lips twitched, but he still turned away, then paused long enough to snap at a uniform standing close by, "Get their statements."

Alex stalked away, leaving them with the uniform, who pulled a notebook and pencil out of his uniform pocket and looked at one and then other.

Becca, biting back a grin, exchanged an amused glance with Zach, who shook his head.

"Kids."

Becca choked.

Oh yeah, they were going to get along fine.

PROCESSIONAL

Zach missed his newspaper. Even though it was easier on the arms and shoulders, a guy couldn't hide behind an electronic tablet in the morning. His old newspaper hid all but his hands, making it like he was invisible. He didn't know why it worked, but he'd gotten the heads up on incoming problems with his kids from behind his newspaper. And it had given him cover if he didn't want to be part of something. With a tablet, you were in the discussion, even if you weren't.

Becca and Nell weren't talking *to* him, but he knew he wasn't out of it. He glanced up. There was one positive. He could look at Becca without being obvious about it. She looked good sitting across from him. It had taken some doing to make it happen.

He'd had to bypass Alex before Alex realized what he was up to—not sure why since Alex had liked Becca. And he'd had to convince Becca and Nell to meet. It felt like Becca made that hard, too. Whatever the reason, it went away when the two women finally met. No more avoiding, in fact, it took a lot of meetings because Nell's problems were big ones. Alex didn't even realize what he'd been saved by his old man. It had been interesting watching—from this side of the table—as Becca slowly began to smooth out the bumps in Nell's wedding road. And while she was doing that, he had eased Becca into the family circle without anyone suspecting his ulterior motives—well, he had a feeling Nell might, but there was no sign she'd said anything to anyone else. He'd know if she had. He might not know much, but he knew his kids, could smell when they were watching him.

And Nell had too much going on to stick her nose into Zach's business. As an only child, he'd wondered how she'd fit into his large and opinionated family, but she'd held her own, hadn't been rolled over by them or her nasty relations. She was good for Alex, though Zach had to remind himself about this whenever her Family cropped up in their lives, either in person or on the news.

Zach was almost content, would be content if it weren't for Alex's efforts to keep him out of the murder investigation into Georgy's death. The boy acted like Zach was a suspect, for Pete's sake. Okay, technically he might be, but he'd arrived after Georgy died. Did Alex think Zach couldn't be impartial about a bunch of people he hadn't seen for fifty years? *Kids.*

He stole a look at Becca. What did she think of his

Baker's Dozen? He'd made sure to introduce them to her gradually, helped by the fact that they'd all been giving the house a wide berth after it had been engulfed in wedding plans. Seemed like she liked them and they liked her, though that might be the relief of slipping out of the wedding planning noose. So far his plan was working. Even if he still had the wedding planning noose around his neck.

Not that they were talking wedding at the moment, he realized. A murder at his class reunion was, apparently, more interesting, even to Nell.

"Hannah told me they suspect his wife," Nell said.

"We—they always look at the spouse," Zach felt impelled to point out.

"Why would she wait to kill him at the reunion?" Nell objected.

"And why would she put him in the memorial display?" Becca added.

Zach shrugged.

"If you were investigating," Becca began, then met his gaze and grinned. "Well, you didn't look too happy when Alex had the guy in uniform take our statements."

Zach set down his tablet, shifting his shoulders. He had been—not happy. He was retired, not senile. He had eyes and instincts. But this was Becca, not Alex, so he smiled and seriously considered her question. Would he have started with Barbara Betty? Probably. "It's not that easy to kill your spouse and not be a suspect," Zach pointed out. "Maybe she hoped it would widen the suspect pool."

Becca nodded thoughtfully. "I guess I can see that, but she was white as a sheet. That's hard to fake."

Barbara Betty had appeared genuinely shocked, though she'd calmed down pretty fast.

"What I don't understand is how no one noticed he was dead for so long." Nell propped her elbows on the table, her eyes bright with curiosity.

Zach enjoyed the glance Becca shot at him, before she said, "In high school if he sat down, he fell asleep. I guess that hasn't—hadn't changed."

"Fifty years," Zach said thoughtfully, remembering now that they got married right out of high school. He'd had eight years with Georgette and nine with Helen. And so many years alone—except for the thirteen kids. Barbara Betty had stuck with old Georgy right up until his expiration date. If she had done it, why now? Why at the reunion? It wasn't unknown for a spouse to snap, but this felt more planned than a snap. He frowned, trying to think like the cop he'd been. Did he want someone else to be guilty because Alex had annoyed him? It was possible. On the other hand, a healthy dose of skepticism was a detective's best friend. Unwanted advice of father to son.

Both women watched him as if they sensed his inner struggle.

"I'm sure Alex is looking at who else might have a motive." He offered this, half with fatherly pride, half with fatherly annoyance. "But killing him at the reunion cuts out anyone who isn't also connected to the class somehow. Georgy and Barbara Betty weren't local." Which would complicate Alex's investigation, Zach thought with some satisfaction. Becca bit her lower lip to hold in a grin, and he gave her a guilty look.

"The catering company?" Becca offered, showing she'd been thinking about that night, too.

"Probably been looked at," he said, just in case Nell told Alex about this conversation, "and they'll take a hard look at who was on either side of Georgy."

"Barbara Betty and Donna May," Becca said. "He dated Donna May before he dated Barbara Betty, but I think she broke up with him when she started hanging out with Lisa Linda. He wasn't the class Biff, but he was close."

"Biff?" Nell's brows rose.

"Class bully," Becca explained, to Zach's relief. He hadn't got the reference either.

"And that mattered...how?" Nell asked.

Becca half turned to Nell. "Lisa Linda was the leader of the in crowd. Head cheerleader, class president, the whole nine yards. I don't know why she picked Donna May, but she did, so Donna May had to date someone else. I think it was one of the football players, a senior who was also Lisa Linda's boyfriend's best friend." She grinned when Nell made a face.

"I guess I was lucky I wasn't in any crowd in high school."

Becca chuckled. "Believe me I wasn't either." Her expression turned thoughtful. "It all seems so far away. All the drama and who was dating who, all that energy expended and for what?"

"Diplomas?" Zach asked with a grin.

"Well, there is that." Becca matched his grin, and his heart thumped hard enough he worried Nell would notice. She sobered. "Is it even remotely possible that something that happened back in high school was the motive?"

"It does feel like a long time to hold a grudge," Nell agreed.

"Was Georgy at any of the other reunions?" Zach asked.

Becca shrugged. "I was neck deep in kids, well," her smile flickered, "it felt like I was, so I didn't go. I could find out, though."

"Is it awful that I'm so gruesomely interested?" Nell asked.

Becca laughed. "That's pretty normal." She leaned forward and said, as if imparting a secret, "I was hoping Alex had shared a few details with you. There, now I'm the awful one."

Nell laughed but shook her head. "The man is a sphinx. Not a single detail. I've had to cull what I can from the news and you two."

"So we don't know if the poison in his food," Becca gave him a hopeful look.

"Alex has steered clear, I presume because I'm also a suspect," Zach said, with only a hint of bitterness.

Nell opened her mouth, then closed it.

"You weren't there when he died," Becca said, then added, "but I'm not in the clear yet." This seemed to make her happy.

"Well, I don't want to be one of those amateur sleuths in the books," Nell said, "but that doesn't mean I'm not curious. Did anyone see him eating his food?"

Zach hesitated, then said, "His plate looked untouched to me, but I didn't see it before."

"There was the mixer before dinner," Becca said, she tapped the fingers of one hand against the table top. "Lots of milling around with plastic cups in our hands. Georgy was awake for that unless he can sleep standing up."

"That would add more suspects to the list, wouldn't it?" Nell asked hopefully.

Alex better hope it was in the food, Zach thought, not as sympathetic as he might have been if he'd been in the loop instead of so far out of the loop, he might as well live in another city.

"Comes down to motive," Zach said. Wasn't in that loop either. If there was a loop.

"I guess no one has mentioned the two deaths before the reunion?" Becca asked. It was her turn to rest her elbows on the table, her chin in her propped hands.

"Two people died before the reunion?" Nell asked,

her eyes widening. Her gaze traveled from Becca to Zach. "Were they murdered, too?"

Zach shrugged. He didn't know if Alex was checking on those two because he hadn't let Zach or Becca tell him about them.

Becca sat back. "While I don't like to bring this up, if this is about us, about our class, why wait until we're already almost, well, gone?"

"It could be a weird coincidence," Nell agreed with some reluctance, "I mean...well, it could be a coincidence."

What she meant was, old people die. Whether they all had one foot in the grave or not, Zach got Becca's point. All the murderer had to do was wait for nature to take its course if the class or some of their classmates were the target. Why risk jail now?

Becca stared straight ahead, her gaze on something out of his sight. He looked at Nell, who gave a tiny shrug, then they both turned to watch Becca. It felt long before she sighed and came to herself again.

"If it was a...a revenge thing," Becca said slowly, "it's someone who wants to get caught. Someone who wants credit."

Zach inhaled sharply. She was right. If the bodies kept piling up, eventually someone would have to notice.

"At first maybe it was enough to kill, but after a while, I think it would get annoying if no one noticed. I mean, the poisoning could be that step, couldn't it?" Becca looked up, glanced from Zach to Nell and, catching something in their expressions, gave a wry smile. "Sorry. I've read too many mysteries."

For just a second, he wondered—but then he looked into her eyes. Man, he could easily get paranoid if he wasn't careful. But she had made him curious. Alex's attitude not withstanding, it wasn't his monkey or his circus. He had—he glanced at a thoughtful Becca—other priorities. Oh, and the wedding.

"We don't know that anyone else has been murdered," he pointed out.

"I can find out." Becca grinned. "Mary Magdalene is still the class newsletter."

Zach hesitated, tempted to try and get the jump on his son. That is if Nell didn't rat them out.

As if she knew, Nell gave a grin that was just a bit evil. "If he asked, I'd have to tell him, but he won't."

Zach chuckled. Dang, the more he got to know Nell the more he liked her.

"I suppose," he said, slowly, "it wouldn't hurt to ask a few careful questions." Now he shot Becca a worried look. "*Careful.* If someone in our class did kill Georgy..." He did not want Becca to pop up on a murderer's radar "...and if Alex found out, well, just be careful."

"I'll be careful," Becca promised, crossing her heart like a kid.

He opened his mouth to reinforce his warning, then closed it again. *Focus, bubba.* While it was true he'd been more tangled in wedding plans than he'd expected, his plan to lure Becca in close was working. It was highly unlikely someone from their class was the killer. Georgy had lived many years away and had all of those years to annoy other people in his life. If playing amateur sleuth helped him spend more time with Becca, well, then he'd play his heart out. He'd managed to spend a lot of time with her the last few weeks, and as far as he could tell, not one of his kids suspected a thing.

"And I'd better get back to my wedding or Alex will smell a rat," Nell said, sliding her lap top over and lifting the lid.

"Oh, that reminds me, Nell," Becca asked, "Did you want the traditional music?"

"Traditional?"

"Prelude, Processional—that's where you march down the aisle—then the interlude, recessional—"

"Where I march back?"

Becca laughed and nodded. "Then the postlude plays while everyone else files out."

Nell looked thoughtful for a moment, then she glanced at Zach and said, "Yeah, let's be traditional. I think my parents would have liked that."

Becca looked down to make a note—and it looked to Zach like she might be blinking back a few tears. For someone with so much Family, Nell was very alone, or she had been.

"I'll email Mary Magdalene and see if I can find out more about Larry Gary and Michael David's deaths," Becca said, pulling out her cell phone. She glanced up from the screen as Zach opened his mouth. "Carefully."

Was her smile filled with that something that said she was not indifferent? Hope was about all he had at his age. He took hope from her lingering smile as she turned her attention to her cell phone.

For a moment, tapping replaced talking, so Zach picked up his tablet and turned the screen back on, but an exclamation from Nell had him looking up.

"That's odd." Nell frowned down at her laptop.

"What?" Becca leaned over to look at the screen.

"The wedding venue refunded my deposit. They said they were sorry to hear about my loss?"

Becca's brows drew together. Even the way she frowned was cute, Zach decided. The frown turned his way, and he straightened. "What loss?"

"I don't know. I'm going to call them." She rose and went into the other room.

Rebecca's frown stayed here with him. "That's the second time that's happened."

"You think someone in her Family is making trouble?" Zach scowled. Had Nell's grandma dearest got out on bail? If the murderous witch was out, one of his kids should have warned them.

Nell came slowly back into the kitchen and sat down by Becca.

"Were you able to get it worked out?" Rebecca put her hand over Nell's.

She used touching a lot, Zach had noticed. Except with him. Once she'd leaned close, laughing, but had stopped just short of touching. That was something he was hoping to change.

Nell's gaze rose with some reluctance to meet Zach's.

Becca stiffened. "Who did they think died?"

She bit her lip, then said, "My father-in-law-to-be."

"But that's—" Becca stopped.

"Me," Zach finished for her. "Interesting."

* * *

The trouble was, it could as easily have been Nell's relatives messing with them as a message from Georgy's killer.

It had been unavoidable for Becca to meet them and they were creepy—and some of them had the requisite dark sense of humor. She'd observed both an Afoniki and a Calvino trying to pull Zach's chain—and sometimes succeeding. But what if this was advance warning from their classmate killer? How did they know the others hadn't been warned?

And how, she wondered, had she gotten in deep enough to feel a clutch of fear at the thought of something happening to Zach?

"You said this wasn't the first time someone messed with your wedding plans?" Zach asked, pulling Becca from her thoughts.

She was not sorry to be pulled. She wasn't living a Hallmark movie—either a romance or a mystery one.

"Someone canceled my flowers." At Zach's frown Nell added, "It was pretty easy to fix."

"We probably need to check with all the vendors," Becca said. If this was one of Nell's Family—Becca had noticed the emphasis Zach used when he talked about them, as opposed to other family and had found herself adding that emphasis to separate the sides—then they needed to nip it in the bud. "Maybe set up a code word for any changes."

"Like spies?" Nell said, a grin replacing her worry.

"Like spies," Becca agreed.

"You'll have to come up with a story or Alex will hear," Zach muttered.

Nell's eyes widened. "But..."

"Of course, you'll tell Alex," she heard Zach's sharp intake as he prepared to protest, but she pressed on, "that someone has been pranking your wedding plans."

"The truth, but not the whole truth?" Nell said doubtfully.

This time Zach didn't move.

"What you feel comfortable with, Nell. You're building a future, not just planning a wedding." She waited a minute, looking for the right way to say it. "And the truth is, we don't know if your wedding has become tangled in his murder investigation."

Nell started to look relieved. "That's true. He'll think it's my Family, too." Now she sounded resigned. "And he's probably right."

She really was a nice person. She had observed that Alex knew he was lucky, she just hoped he'd keep remembering and keep on being the man Nell deserved. Alex was the only one of Zach's kids who had kept their distance from her. He'd been polite enough, but definitely aloof. Of course, that could be because he was looking into their class for the killer and he had to treat her as a suspect. And if she were a suspect, he wouldn't like her getting cozy with his family, or in particular, his Nell.

Nell looked at her list and then sighed, giving Zach a sly look. "Maybe we should just elope to Vegas. We could get married by a fake Elvis."

Becca laughed and saw a grin chase away Zach's frown.

"Well, as fun as that would be, let's see how messed up your arrangements actually are. I can help with that." She picked up her cell phone. "Which ones do you want me to call?"

"Did you lose your venue? You could always fall back on Sarah's house, couldn't you?" Zach suggested.

Becca had met Sarah, of course. She was good people, too.

"And fill her house with a bunch of perps?" Nell's expression lightened.

They all laughed, releasing most, if not all the tension in the room.

"If you'll do these," Nell said, showing her the list on her laptop, "I'll do the bottom half."

Becca pulled out her cheaters, turning the blurs into text she could see. As she dialed, her thoughts circled around to wondering why she still felt worried. It was normal, natural even, she told herself. It was her job to worry and to anticipate trouble, so it could be smoothed out before it toppled Nell's plans. Even if she hadn't come to know Zach and his family, she'd have been worried about him, but...

Would she have been this worried? She wanted to call Alex herself and order him to look after his dad. She wanted—she looked around the battered kitchen, scoured down almost completely to the wood by the years when Zach's horde had inhabited this place. Say they did...become interested. Play it out to the end, Becca, she told herself. Two seventy-plus year olds getting married? With his thirteen and her three plus in-laws in the mix?

It didn't matter if they were all adults. It was one reason why she'd never dated after her husband died. She'd picked their father out and had lucked out because they'd both been young. But when he died, she was old enough to know how much luck had played in the picking. And she hadn't trusted herself to pick their step-father. She should know. Her mother had remarried. Becca hadn't hated him, but she hadn't liked how help-less she felt, how lost. They'd gotten past it, and she'd sincerely mourned him when he passed, but...she didn't want to do that to her kids.

Who weren't kids. But were, and always would be, her kids.

And if that wasn't enough...*Marriage.* It was about a lot more than the kids getting along with a new step something.

She looked up and caught Zach looking at her. So,

she hadn't imagined it. She wasn't sixteen anymore, wondering if this boy or that liked her. She was a woman. An old woman, she inserted firmly. Old enough to know when a man wasn't interested.

And when he was.

What she hadn't expected was to like it.

* * *

He couldn't say that Nell didn't have a sense of humor about her Family. He liked the way it put the smile back in Becca's eyes, even if it was only for a minute. She was worried about him. That was a good sign. If he knew who'd played the prank, he might have sent them a thank you note. Was it time to make his move? He'd been circling the woman for what felt like forever. At their age, it kind of was.

Nell rose with her phone and went into the living room again, but Becca stayed at the table, dialing the pastor who was to perform the ceremony, he decided, based on Becca's side of the conversation.

A frown pulled her brows together. "No, there's been no death in the family."

So whoever it was had tried it with the padre, too. His money was still on Nell's Family—though he didn't mind Becca worrying about him. Worry had trapped more than one woman in a relationship. Zach didn't have any illusions about being a catch. He hadn't been a catch when he was young, sure wasn't one now. But he'd seen guys in worse shape than him reel a woman in.

Becca's next call, the photographer, he figured, was

the same. Someone had called and told them there'd been a death. His death, if her wide-eyed worry was any indication.

He frowned. Was this a warning shot across his bow? He didn't think about dying that much. He'd lived a good life. Had done more than he ever thought he would. And he couldn't say his name would die out, not with thirteen kids. But he sure as heck didn't want anyone ending it before his time. Or before he got to get his arms around Becca and found out if he could still kiss a woman. If someone was reaching out from the past to kill him? Well, he'd been a stubborn old goat long before he became a stubborn old goat.

INTERLUDE

Becca wasn't quite sure how she'd ended up having dinner alone with Zach. Not in his house either. Out in public. Like a date having dinner.

It had been so many years since she'd been out like this with someone who was not her husband. It was ridiculous for a grown—grown old—woman to be nervous. And she wasn't exactly nervous. The truth was, she didn't know how she felt because she wasn't sure this was a date. It looked like a date, he smelled like a date—yummy—and this place looked like a date place, with shadowy nooks and more yummy smells. She was pretty sure it was a date, but not sure enough to say the words out loud.

What perhaps surprised her the most was how she and Zach had become friends in the few weeks since the reunion. In many ways, it felt like they'd been friends all along. It all happened so naturally that, well, she wasn't quite sure how it happened.

"You don't know how it was for anyone else back then, do you?" Zach said, lowering his menu so he could look at her.

For a minute, Becca was lost, then it clicked. "In high school? No." She shook her head. No one had known about her secret yearnings for Zach and she sure hadn't known she was not alone in her secret yearnings. It would be easier, at this point, to identify someone who hadn't had a secret crush on him, she decided, with an inner grin. If such a girl existed.

"We just spun in our own orbits," he mused, a slight frown not putting the slightest dent in his cute factor.

She refused to even think the word hot because the only hot in her life was hot flashes.

"Too self-centered to know how self-centered we were," she agreed. She smiled at the girl she'd been, knew she couldn't completely, well, she could remember how it was, but she couldn't put herself back in that Becca's mind and feel what she'd felt. She glanced at Zach, well, she could feel that again, the old crush, but not the other. Once she'd left self-absorption behind, there was no going back. Which was probably a good thing. So much drama and heart burning. The extremes that made her tired just thinking about it. "And," she added, her thoughts drifting back to her heart burnings for Zach, "so afraid someone might find out how we felt and taunt us about it."

He nodded. "I remember that. Gotta be tough. Show no fear."

"Real men don't cry." Almost hesitantly her gaze connected with his. It felt like he was headed somewhere. Was this about Georgy's murder or—

Without her realizing it was within his reach, his hand covered hers on the table.

"I looked at you," he said, "back then, but I didn't know how to talk to you."

Becca felt herself jerk and wondered if he felt the jerk. Her heart sped up. Had her doctor missed something at her last checkup?

"You always seemed so..." his voice trailed off.

She wanted to ask him, "so what?" but her throat was too dry. She picked up her water glass with her free hand, but lowered it without drinking because she couldn't, didn't want to break the lock his eyes had on hers.

"Up," he finally said. "Like the," he cleared his throat, "clouds. Like something I could see, but couldn't reach."

Becca knew her jaw dropped, but she couldn't seem to do anything about it. No wonder he'd managed to persuade two women to marry him and have kids with him. She blinked. It was a good thing that ship had sailed for her.

"I came to the reunion to see you."

She had to blink because her eyeballs were crying out for moisture. She touched the side of his hand with her thumb, rubbed the rough skin. She'd forgotten what it was like to hold hands with a man. She looked away, gathered her courage and met his gaze again.

"I...noticed you, too," she admitted. The world did not stop turning. Stars didn't fall out of the sky. No mountains turned into lakes. But she knew something had changed. Somewhere inside she might be afraid, but it wasn't possible to be afraid while Zach held onto her hand. She could fall—without falling.

His mouth started to turn up—and their waiter chose that moment to come back.

They probably looked ridiculous in his young eyes. He didn't know that life, that feeling didn't stop just because your body slowed down. With a flicker of a smile, Zach pulled his hand back and picked up the menu again. "Are you ready?"

She nodded, not sure what he was asking. Later she might be embarrassed, but right now she was hungry. She gave her order and handed over her menu, then waited for Zach. When they were alone again, for some reason, what might be happening with them made her think about Georgy.

"What if Georgy's death was...was..." she stopped, not sure how to put it.

"About someone thinking one thing and Georgy not having a clue?"

She nodded, grateful he hadn't made it personal. "You said something the other night about a trigger? What would trigger a, a killing spree? Or a killing," she amended. Mary Magdalene had supplied the missing details, but they didn't provide clarity. James John had crashed his car into a tree, and Larry Gary had had a heart attack. And exactly a week after the reunion, Frank Ray Saint-Marc had died from food poisoning. Not exactly a neon arrow pointing to a murder rampage, but the dates were troubling. "We're all dying."

His grin flickered again. After a moment, his gaze narrowed. "If the murderer was dying...?"

Becca stiffened. "It might not be enough that people died, not if you died first?"

"It's a possibility. Not that Alex would be interested. There's not enough there. If our perp is there in our past, he or she isn't trying that hard to out themselves."

So much for her theory that the murderer wanted credit. Her thoughts began to spin a little. She absently picked up the bread the waiter had left, buttered it and took a bite, chewing slowly. When she swallowed, she looked at the bread, then at Zach. "That's really good."

He nodded as if satisfied.

All the girls had a crush on Zach. But if this was about Zach, why kill anyone else? Unless Georgy was the only victim? "Everyone knew you'd RSVP'd to come to the reunion," she said. She took another bite and chewed slowly. Zach, to his credit, didn't ask her what on earth she was talking about. He just waited, watching her in that intent way she was coming to know, coming to...like...

"All the girls had a crush on Zach," she murmured

when she'd swallowed and had a drink. "That's what Bettina said at the reunion."

"You think this is about me?"

"What if the other deaths were just that? Accidents? They could have given our murderer an idea. Georgy's death was a way to get your attention? If she was dying—
"

"We've gone from he or she to a positive she?" He protested.

"Well, I guess it could be a man crush..."

"So she is trying to get my attention?" he cut in. He was quiet for a moment, then he sighed. "You know we're just...just..."

"Talking to each other? Have absolutely no power to do anything about it?" She gave him a sympathetic look, and she didn't say, "Welcome to my world." Which she thought it was very grown-up of her.

* * *

Zach didn't talk much after their food came. His mother taught him not to eat with his mouth full, and he had a lot to think about. Most of it was about Becca.

She'd noticed *him*. Man, he hadn't been tempted to go back in time and be a teen again, but she almost tempted him. If he could know what he knew now. Since he couldn't go back in time, he didn't want to lose time now. But he could tell Becca had gone as far as she could tonight. She ate her food almost primly, but every so often she'd look at him like she expected to find him gone.

He'd take it as a good sign, a hopeful sign.

And he was willing to keep chewing on the edges of the murder and getting nowhere if they could do it together. Otherwise, he was over Georgy's death.

Finally, Becca put her fork down and leaned back with a sigh of contentment that reminded him he was still a guy with guy urges. He'd been kind of worried about that.

"I suppose Alex is still..."

"Avoiding me? Like the plague. Thinks because I'm retired my brain is out to pasture, too." Not that he'd want to take any of their deductions to Alex and prove him right. Would have been interesting to see the facts in the case, though. He'd always liked puzzles. "Kids." He almost snorted but managed to stop himself. "How about your kids? They treat you like you're senile?"

"Mine are all overseas for the present, so they aren't up in my, er, grill."

That made him smile. He liked a woman who could make him smile. "You miss them."

She nodded, even though it hadn't been a question. "But...I'm not integral to their lives. They are doing great, and they love it when I visit, but to them..."

"You're on pause when they aren't in the room," Zach finished.

She laughed. "To some extent, yes. And it should be that way. They shouldn't be weighed down by me. I wanted them to have wings, so I'm glad they use them. Even if I sometimes have to remind myself to be glad."

"It's uncomfortable, isn't it, the hard truth?" He hesitated. "Your parents?"

"They lived long enough to know my kids, and so I could tell them I'm sorry."

He laughed at that. "I probably should have done that."

"Well, you were busy. Did your kids know their grandparents?"

"Not really. Alex may remember them." He hadn't made sure his kids knew any of their grandparents. He'd been so busy, and then they'd been gone. It wasn't until Nell skidded into their lives that he'd thought much about extended family. He cleared his throat. "Do you want dessert?"

She shook her head, and as if he sensed the table might clear for the next round of patrons, their waiter appeared with the bill. Zach handed him a credit card.

"I really enjoyed the dinner, Zach. Thank you."

"I enjoyed it, too. Thank you for coming."

There was a short silence that did not bother Zach, since he spent it looking at Becca. It wasn't just about *a* woman. It was pleasure at the sight of her. Maybe another night, if he could talk her into it, he'd sit next to her where they could touch, but for now, he wanted to look.

"Becca?" A pause and then with rising curiosity, "Zach Baker?"

Becca gave a start, her head jerking toward the voice. He looked more slowly.

"Dot?"

Becca clearly hadn't been expecting her. He was watching her close enough to see the effort it took for her to smile.

"How on earth did you get...here?" Becca tossed her napkin down and rose so they could fake hug. Zach stood up, too, because he'd been raised that way.

"Coming here for the reunion, well, it just brought it all back. New Orleans. Home. I went back and was so miserable, and then I realized, I can do what I want. Go where I want. So here I am."

Though the tone was happy, her face didn't seem able to manage that much expression. She was like one of those frontier rag dolls with just a bit of the features stitched on.

"You're...moving back to New Orleans?" Becca's shock was shy of happy.

"Sold my house and I'm staying in an apartment until I find a new one." Her gaze flicked to Zach. "Old friends are the best friends, don't you think?"

He made a noncommittal sound because he and Becca hadn't been friends in the past. He hoped Dot wasn't planning on taking up with Becca where they left off. He hadn't cared for Dot back then, and she had not improved with time.

The waiter brought the receipt for Zach to sign, which he did quickly, adding more tip than he would have because it made the math simpler and faster. He stepped away from the table, reaching over to hand

Becca her purse. He glanced around suggestively, and Dot's smile grew wider and thinner.

"My party is over there. Nice to see you both. Such a surprise. I didn't realize you knew each other..." Her voice trailed off, but Zach didn't wait for it to trail back up.

He knew how to move people from one place to another.

"Let's do lunch, Becca!" Dot called after her.

Becca managed a half wave as Zach hurried them toward the exit. He waited for her to protest, but she didn't say anything until they were standing outside waiting for the car to be brought around.

"That's...odd," she said, staring straight head for several minutes. Then she looked at him and grinned a bit ruefully. "I think Georgy's murder is making me paranoid."

Zach glanced around. It was New Orleans at night, so they weren't alone, but it was New Orleans at night, so it didn't matter. A couple of steps back and they'd be in shadow. He took her arm and drew her slowly out of the entrance lights. Her eyes widened, but she didn't resist.

Maybe she was as curious as he was to find out what a first kiss would be like at their age. He didn't grab her or anything. They didn't have much time before the car would be here. He rested one hand on her shoulder, used the other to tip her chin up and bent his head to hers.

Before contact, her scent flooded his senses with old memories and new hope. It had been a long time, but he was glad to find out he still knew how. That the magic could still happen. His hand cupping her chin felt her pulse speed up, so he knew she felt it, too.

He heard footsteps and lifted his head, brushing her hair back with a hand that might have trembled before he stepped back and turned to face the kid who didn't have his car.

"We're sorry, sir. Someone slashed your tires. We've called a service..." his voice rattled on, but Zach quit listening as Becca's hand gripped his arm.

He covered her hand with his and squeezed it as her worried gaze met his. He shook his head, but he had to admit, instincts he'd thought were dormant had just given a little twitch. Not a full on kick. But a warning to watch his back, just the same.

*　*　*

Becca fluffed the skirt of Nell's wedding dress and stepped back. Functioning as a quasi-wedding planner had not been in the playbook but she'd enjoyed it. With three sons, she'd not been a mother of any bride. Ellie, Nell's long lost not-evil grandma, was super sweet and Becca had been careful not to step on her toes. But it was clear the two were still feeling their way in a relationship that was new to them both.

A lot like she and Zach.

Dating. She was over seventy years old, and she was dating. That night, after Zach's tires had been fixed and he'd taken her home, after he'd kissed her goodnight—with a lot of confidence and skill, she'd conceded—she'd gone into her empty house, donned her granny pj's and stared at herself in the mirror, trying reconcile the outward person with the inside one.

I'm too old, she told herself. We're too old. The thought hadn't helped that much. When you were young, you didn't know anything about getting old. You didn't know that the outside and the inside got disconnected and out of synch. That inside her old body was this young person wondering what the crap had happened. Someone who could, apparently, still feel young things despite the broken-down exterior.

She had the urge to flee, but her aging exterior couldn't. It was so undignified and where would she go? She was home, and Zach knew where she lived. She half laughed, then bit her lip as fear tried to get a foothold.

"You've faced harder things that getting the hots for an old crush, old woman." It wasn't fear of the unknown, she'd realized, but the known. She remembered what it was like to not be alone.

The sounds of someone else in the house. Being needed and needing.

Hugging. Kissing...

She felt a chill take the edge off warm, though it couldn't quite dispel it when she could still remember the feel of Zach holding her close. It had felt so good and so terrifying. Because...

Sex.

Her insides might be young, but her outside had taken a lot of damage. It sagged in places she didn't like seeing, sure wouldn't like being seen. A muffin top was the reality she lived with, but could sometimes forget while wearing her control top jeans. You couldn't wear control top anything while making love.

Love. Was that what she felt or something else? She didn't want to call it lust because of her old exterior and her dignity, which was almost all she had left. But it was hard to lie to herself when she remembered what love felt like, too.

She'd just never expected to feel it again.

Nell gave a sedate twirl, making the knee length skirt fan out. She stopped facing Becca, an anxious look in her eyes.

"You look beautiful," Becca assured her, the slight quiver in her voice for Nell, taking her first steps into love and for herself—afraid to try it again.

Nell's chin lifted, and her smile bloomed. That smile, Becca decided, was how Alex fell. It turned on a light inside Nell like night turning to day. And then it faded and shadows appeared in her eyes.

"I'm really nervous," she admitted, stepping down so that they were eye-to-eye. "Alex, his family. My family..." Her words trailed off, and she grimaced.

Becca knew this part, knew the right words, but this time they had a double meaning. She gripped Nell's hands and waited for Nell to meet her gaze.

"Love is not for the faint of heart, Nell, it's a leap into

the unknown. You don't get to see what you're getting when you commit your life to someone. You fall together and if you hang on," her voice faltered for a moment because hanging on didn't work when your love died, but she pushed that back, because loss was part of the leap, part of what you couldn't know. And if she'd known? She'd have leaped again rather than not have the memories, the love, the learning, the children, all of it. "If you hang on to each other, you'll be all right." She hesitated because this time she might have been talking to herself, "It's the times when you don't do something because you're afraid that you regret the most."

Nell's smile came back, but the look in her eyes told Becca she'd sensed that the words weren't just for her bridal nerves. She looked like she wanted to ask, but the clerk came into the fitting room.

"How are we doing?" she asked brightly.

Becca arched a brow at Nell and got a nod.

"We're doing just fine, thanks."

If she said it enough times, Becca might even believe it.

Nell waited until they were alone again and presented her back so Becca could free her from the dress, but she looked over her shoulder to ask, "Anything new on the murder?"

Becca hesitated, then shook her head.

"I suppose Alex is still keeping mum about it?" Becca asked.

"Luckily we have other things to talk about, or we

would just sit and stare at each other over dinner," Nell said with a laugh.

Becca hesitated, trying to decide how to ask, but Nell must have read her face.

"And no, he hasn't asked about the wedding plans. Since we got the mischief stopped, well," she shrugged.

Becca turned to hang up Nell's dress so she couldn't read her expression this time. The mischief hadn't stopped but switched to Zach. Of course, that assumed it was the same person who had done both. Based on her vast experience as an armchair, mystery-reading detective, it didn't feel like the same person. Or it was someone who'd lost control? The slashing of Zach's tires felt like an angry act, while the other things were more like the drip of water on rock. Carefully planned to annoy. Georgy's murder had to have been planned, based on the memorial, unless someone had seen it and used it?

She wanted to grab the sides of her head. Too many thoughts, too many what-ifs and wherefores and no access to any real information.

"Well, as long as no one else has died..." Nell's voice trailed off.

Neither Zach nor Alex would thank her for mentioning Frank Ray. And food poisoning happened. As did heart attacks and people who hit trees with their cars. While she hadn't asked, she had a feeling Zach hadn't told his kids about his slashed tires or the other stuff. She had the feeling he was humoring her by "investigating" with her so that they could spend non-wedding planning time together. Except...every now and again he'd get what she called his cop look. Like the look, he'd given her when she suggested the killer might want to get caught. She was pretty sure that for a few seconds at least, he'd suspected her. And he still wanted to date her. If their relationship made it, well, further, she was so going to pay him back for that.

Becca turned around and gave Nell a grin. "Well, I've not lost anyone during a wedding, though it has been close a couple of times."

Nell laughed, then turned to pick up her purse. "So, what's our next stop?"

"Florist final check and then caterer final check."

Neither one of them commented on the fact that the code words had worked. Their prankster had tried it on one more time and then faded away.

Or targeted Zach. But why?

Every question came back to why?

* * *

When Becca posed the question to Zach later, mostly to get that look of longing out of his eyes, he pretended to give it careful consideration.

Finally, he said, "Sometimes people don't have a reason for what they do. Sometimes, they just do things."

"Impulse control problems?" Killers with this problem didn't show up a lot in cozy mysteries because impulsive killers were impulsive and random, making sleuthing them out difficult for author and reader. She liked the clues, the building suspense, and hated a mystery that took her all the way to the end, and then brought in a ringer killer who hadn't been on the page through the whole book. Now in real life, it probably happened a lot.

Zach nodded, and the look seeped back into his eyes. It was all the wedding stuff in the air. It was giving him ideas, and none of their kids knew they were dating. Which either said something about how devious they'd managed to be, or how clueless the kids in question were. Becca couldn't even give her kids a pass for being out of the country because she'd had a lot more trouble video chatting with them the past month. She could tell her daughters-in-law were catching on, but her boys had flies buzzing over their heads.

If someone had noticed, they might have thought it was fear of losing another husband that held her back, but that wasn't that at all. Becca hadn't managed to mentally get herself from holding hands across a candle-lit table, and heated kisses on her stoop to the, well, the honeymoon. Night after night, they'd kiss goodnight— and the kisses were getting longer and warmer—and she'd go into her lonely house all dreamy and soft and thinking she was all that and then she'd see herself in the mirror, and it was bucket of cold water to the face time.

It was one thing to start out young and hot, well hottish, to age with someone gradually, both of you growing old together. Fate had stripped her of that, so she'd moved on. Pushed desire to the back burner and let it grow cold.

When she was with Zach, he made her feel young and yes, hot again. She couldn't lie to her lined face or her saggy body. She'd pined for him in high school, and now she was as hot for him now as she could at her age. Not just for hugs and snuggles. She wanted to get naked with him without getting naked with him. She could insist on a total blackout, but she couldn't hide forever. And it was only going to get worse. Gravity didn't miss a minute dragging her stuff down.

If they were different people, they'd have done something to get over the hurdle, but they were who they were.

The marrying kind of people.

So the naked elephant kept getting bigger and bigger. Why didn't guys worry about that? She had a feeling that for Zach, all he waited on was Alex and Nell's wedding.

It sent a shiver down her back when he looked at her. Followed by a chill.

"Well, as I live and die, look who is here. And together."

Zach gave her a rueful look before they both turned to see Lisa Linda and Donna May.

She was surprised they hadn't run into them sooner. Lisa Linda liked to say she was "everywhere," like a credit card or an airline.

Without being asked, they pulled out the empty

chairs and sat down, both resting elbows on the table, chins on elbows.

"How *long* has this been going on?" Lisa Linda asked, her gaze danced between Becca and Zach.

Zach met her gaze with Zach-like calm. Becca felt her cheeks heat a little, but she'd learned how to hold her own.

"Dit*to*," Donna May said, somehow managing to sound more like an echo than a person. She batted her lashes at Zach and tried for demure.

Failed, but she tried.

Scarlet tipped fingers reached out for one of Becca's fries. When Lisa Linda lifted the fry up so her matching scarlet lips could close around it, Becca shot a look at Zach and then had to stop her lips from twitching at how stoic he looked. He'd been a cop and father to thirteen, so yeah, bet stoic was his go to place. She glanced at Lisa Linda, and she winked, causing Becca even more difficulty not laughing.

"You two could be a comedy act," Zach said.

The two pointed at each other and then laughed. Lisa Linda leaned back. "How come we didn't know this before the reunion. It's almost as interesting as Georgy."

"I think it's more interesting," Donna May said.

"Anything else interesting happening with the class?" Zach asked casually.

It was only because she knew that Becca shot him a quick look. She'd make a lousy detective she decided. Never learned poker, so no poker face.

"No one else has died, if that's what you're asking," Lisa Linda said, almost regretfully.

"They say Bubba Pascal probably won't make it," Donna May pointed out.

"What happened to Bubba?" Becca asked. It had been Bubba who "woke" Georgy up at the reunion.

"Fell off a ladder or something," Donna May said, vaguely. "His wife messaged Mary Magdalene so she could let could let the class know."

"We're dropping like flies lately," Lisa Linda said, helping herself to another fry.

"Who's dropping like flies?" another voice joined the conversation.

Dot.

Becca had not been able to mesh her schedule with her old friend, but this was the third time they'd run into her accidentally. Dot snagged a chair from a nearby table and eased herself in when Donna May gave an inch or two on one side and Becca on her other.

And just in case things were quite ridiculous enough, Becca heard, "Dad?" off to the right.

At least they didn't look like they were out on a date. She glanced at the two plates. Well, not much. She edged her plate, so it was halfway between her and Dot as Alex closed on them. Alex and Nell.

Alex's gaze traveled around the table, but Becca wasn't sure if he was looking at people or plates. As if to help them, Dot took a couple of Becca's fries, then helped herself to a fried shrimp.

With increased stoicism, Zach introduced everyone. Nell gave Becca a sympathetic look, and then the inevitable uncomfortable silence built.

It lasted until Dot began to gasp and clutch her throat.

RECESSIONAL

Dot hadn't died. Apparently, she was allergic to the shrimp. Or something on the shrimp. So probably nothing to do with their non-investigation or vague suspicions.

Somehow Becca found she'd been co-opted to pick Dot up from the hospital the next morning. She would have offered but felt manipulated and annoyed as Zach drove her home. Instead of murder thoughts, she found herself thinking about stalking. Was she too suspicious? But she'd always told her kids to trust their instincts.

"If you feel uneasy, there is a reason," was her mantra to them and herself as a woman living alone.

Since moving to New Orleans, Dot had tried to cling. Dot had failed, partly because Becca was very involved in Nell's wedding and partly because she didn't like clinging. Dot's random appearances where she and Zach had been eating, well, up to now they had been a minor annoyance. Dot could show up, but they didn't have to invite her to join them. It was, however, interesting that she showed up again and got sick.

It could be a coincidence.

But it smelled like something else, and not just barf.

Zach stopped his car in front of Becca's house but made no move to climb out.

"I don't like it," he said, then glanced at her with the look of a man prepared to argue his point.

"I don't either." At his look of surprise, she added, "I need good instincts in my business." Had honed them while raising three boys as a widow, she could have added. Instead, she said, "It's all so disconnected. Georgy's murder, the sort of timed deaths, and Dot."

"Do you suspect her?" Zach asked bluntly.

"Of murder? I can't think of any reason she'd have to murder Georgy." Becca was quiet for a minute. "It's just weird. All these pieces were floating around, but they all seem to be from a different, well, puzzle. I keep feeling like somewhere there is a connection." And there was sort of. If she took out the attempts to mess up Nell's wedding, there was the fact they were from the same graduating class. If she added Nell back in, there was a loose connecting thread to Zach. Dot had had a crush on him, too. But if this was about Zach, then that snipped the connecting threads to Georgy and the others. It was also possible, she thought ruefully, that the CEO of *Creative Solutions* was having a hard time separating herself from the mystery-reading, armchair detective.

"A murder investigation can be like that," Zach said, adding hastily, "not that this is. I'm just saying, investigations in general, can be chaotic until the right pieces start to fall into place."

"How does that happen?" Becca asked, a bit despondently.

"You start to glimpse the perp, get a hint of what drives him or her." He hesitated again. "And sometimes all you see is...is..."

"*Through a glass darkly?*" Becca offered.

He shot her a look. "Yeah. You know it, but you can't put all the pieces together."

"Do you feel like our pieces could be put together?"

He was quiet for a while. Becca liked that he took his time, that he gave her question serious thought. Or he made it look like he was giving it serious thought. She knew he'd been humoring her through some of their "investigating." She'd even figured out why. Guys could be such guys. And we let them, she admitted. Sometimes we let them because it's cute and sweet.

He sighed and rubbed his face. "Honestly? I think it feels connected because of the reunion."

That made sense. Becca nodded slowly. "Because we re-connected, it all feels connected."

"If we could find some other link, something more recent, or something shared by all the victims..." he trailed off. Then he scowled. "The kind of information you get when you're not a retired cop. And it's your case."

Becca inched a bit closer and covered this hand where it gripped the steering wheel. She waited until he looked at her.

"Would you have listened to you if you were Alex?"

His gaze narrowed, but that's all she could see with his in the shadow. However, the essence of him was a strong presence in the close confines of the car. Her thoughts shifted from murder to romance. To wondering how she could get from where she was—in body issues land—to where she'd like to be—with Zach. She'd like for them to climb out of the car together and, still chatting, walk to their house hand-in-hand. Sometimes she could convince herself it didn't matter—all of those times when she wasn't looking at her saggy self in a mirror. Maybe she should get rid of all her mirrors. Never look in one again.

She'd been...shy on her wedding night the first time John had touched her. She'd gotten over it pretty fast, but back then her stuff wasn't sagging into a doughy mess around her middle. All her stuff had been where it was supposed to be. Gravity wasn't just something that kept her from flying off into space.

Zach gave a wry laugh, breaking into her hot, but cold thoughts. "No, I probably wouldn't have listened to me. Still don't like it."

"No, we still don't like it," she agreed.

* * *

Nell's bridal shower did not help Becca's body-image issues. Though Nell considered Becca a guest—

which she planned to be when the cake came out—she was seated slightly behind Nell as she opened the presents, which were mostly variations of naughty nightwear. The kind that would ruthlessly highlight Becca's saggy bits if she were crazy enough to put any of it on those saggy bits.

Someone should design old-body naughty stuff, she decided, as she matched a name to a negligee that was constructed almost without fabric. The edible nightie Nell opened next made Becca feel a hundred years old until she tried to imagine Zach—or her late husband, John—eating a nightie. A giggle bubble formed in her throat. She managed to hold it back, but not the grin. No one was looking at her anyway.

She looked up from her notebook and realized someone was looking at her.

Becca had been surprised to find Bettina Bailey and Mary Joanne Rivet on Sarah's guest list for the shower. Apparently, they were both Sarah's clients and were also loosely related to Nell's St. Cyr side. The law abiding side, they'd carefully pointed out when Becca hadn't asked them.

"I had to include them," Sarah explained, "or they were going to bail Nell's grandma dearest out of jail."

Law-abiding with blackmail tendencies, Becca noted.

The more time Becca spent with Sarah, the more she liked her, even if she was tall, blonde, young, and thin. After a few minutes in her company, Becca forgot how perfect she was and just enjoyed her, except at bridal showers, of course.

Now she caught Bettina looking at her and wondered if she were as desperate to leave as Becca. And why she'd wanted to come so badly. From across the room, it was hard to imagine Bettina connected to anything but a family Bland, instead of a Family Empire —while ruefully conceding that Bettina's doughy exterior was very similar to her own. Sitting next to her, Mary Joanne had tried harder to fight the ravages of time. Time had noticed, Becca decided and found other ways to telegraph Mary Joanne's age. She was narrow and long, the overly tanned skin stretched paper thin on her visible bones—and the not visible ones, Becca had to assume. Her overly bleached hair was carefully styled so as to not look carefully styled. Mary Joanne was telling her "seventy is the new sixty" story to a couple of Zach's daughters—who were still too young to understand.

The presents all opened, Becca sat back with a sigh of relief. Maybe the twenty years she'd lost seeing and cataloging this stuff would come back. If there was cake.

She noticed that Nell, the gift opening done, had leaned back in her chair, her gaze turning dreamy and her hands air sketching—like as not—her guests into vegetables or fruits, though sometimes she sketched people as people Becca had learned. She made a mental note to ask Nell in a few days if she could to see the sketches. Would the children's book author put them in naughty underwear?

"How about some cake?" Sarah said, sending sighs of happiness—relief?—around the room.

Over the heads of her guests, Sarah gave her a wink, just as *All You Need is Love* began to filter into the room. Becca almost snorted out her nose. It had been on the reunion playlist for after dinner but, well, stuff had happened.

Across the room, Becca saw Bettina and Mary Joanne watching her. It was a little unnerving, so she rose and walked across the room.

"Cake?" Becca arched her brows. If they hadn't been so opposite, Becca would have said the way their lips tipped up in sort of smiles was sort of identical.

"You never said how you know dear Nell," Bettina said plaintively.

"Didn't I?" She tempted to leave it at that, but they probably already knew. "Zach introduced us. She's very nice, isn't she?"

Both gazes switched to where Nell was taking a piece of cake from Sarah. Then the gazes switched back.

"Yes," Mary Joanne said, "she's very nice."

Her tone was the right amount of warm, so it puzzled Becca why her words didn't feel like a compliment.

* * *

Other than Logan Ferris, Alex's bachelor party guests were all related. This was good, Zach decided, since the party had no stripper to jump out of a cake, no booze, and no questionable movies. Zach knew his presence was part of the reason, but even without him, Alex had no interest in strippers or questionable movies, and his years as a street cop had cured him of any desire to drink. His brothers did not seem to mind. It wasn't easy to get them all in the same room, and they were enjoying just talking to each other. And Logan Ferris didn't dare mind, not with Zach watching him.

Thankfully, Alex had no objections to food, or his dad would have to kick his butt out of New Orleans. And because this was New Orleans, the food more than made up for any other lack. Not that Zach wanted strippers or beer.

He needed to keep his wits about him. There'd been a couple more incidents that he had not told Becca about. The gal had a big imagination, though Zach was beginning to wonder if it was her instincts and not her imagination. Someone had bumped him into the street at a light last Friday. Good thing the driver of the car that almost hit him had good reflexes. And one of those systems that helped cars break.

And tonight, crossing the street to the party, a car had roared out of a dark alley and almost hit him. He might still be feeling a bit of adrenaline from leaping up on the curb. The driver had veered like he or she wanted to jump the curb, but you didn't do that in this part of town. Not with the metal strips that lined the very high curbs. It had slid along the curve—which had most likely sliced the tires, causing it to wobble wildly out of sight. Was it significant or a coincidence that it was once again a Friday? And, if Friday mattered to the possible perp, why? Was it male hubris to suspect a woman, based on the driving?

He sipped his soft drink and considered the question and decided it wasn't. It wasn't the bad driving, but a strength issue. Wasn't that easy to bring a car back under control after hitting something and popping a tire, particularly at the speed it had been traveling. His gaze drifted to his boys, clustered together around the food table. They'd apparently decided it was easier to graze than go back and forth.

At the edge, in the group but not of the group, was Ferris, Hannah's boyfriend, and Alex's partner. After a hesitation, Ferris walked over and dropped in the seat across from Zach.

Zach tried not to scowl at him. He wasn't a bad guy. He'd liked him before he started dating Hannah. And he knew that other guys dated his other daughters. But it was intellectual knowledge because his daughters had kept them far away from their dad. He didn't mind. If he didn't have to see them, then they weren't real.

Ferris was real.

Ferris lifted his cup and sipped from his straw, glanced back at Alex and crew, then cleared his throat. "So Hannah told me that Nell said something that made her think that Alex and I might be missing something in the Guidry murder."

It took Zach a minute to parse out this carefully

neutral non-question. "I wouldn't know," he finally said. "I'm retired."

A smile flickered on Ferris's face. "Oh, Alex. He does not make it easy."

Zach might have resented this, but truth was truth.

"What if I was to drop by to pick your brain for the best man's speech? Later tonight? Or tomorrow? I could use some insider info on Alex."

His intent gaze seemed to be saying he might have more than questions about Alex, so Zach nodded. "Sure." His gaze flicked toward the food. "This party probably won't outlast the gumbo."

Ferris chuckled. "Don't expect it will." He glanced at the boys again. "Nice to see them together. They grumble about each other so much, you forget they like each other."

* * *

Zach was quiet when he picked Becca up for the rehearsal dinner. Becca shot him a quick glance as he settled behind the steering wheel. The furrow between his bristling gray brows was deep, and his lips were compressed. She knew none of them had tied it on last night at the bachelor's party. So that couldn't be it.

When she was younger, she would have wondered if she'd done something. She knew she hadn't done anything. She smiled a bit for her younger, drama-prone self. If Zach wanted to bail on this, whatever if was, then he would tell her flat out. And if he did? How would she feel? She didn't want to go there. There was no point because she didn't think he was cooling on them. When he picked her up, he hadn't kissed her like a guy who was cooling.

And this was their "coming out." They were going into the dinner together. Like a couple. Because they were a couple. In front of God and his kids. If he'd changed his mind, he wouldn't have picked her up.

That left a problem between the bride and groom. But her grapevine in the Baker family was pretty good. And Nell would have called her. So not the happy couple.

So that left...

"Logan Ferris came over last night," Zach said suddenly as if he'd been waiting for her to go through the mental checklist.

Becca started to say, "Hannah's guy" but changed it to, "Alex's partner."

"He brought the file on Georgy's murder."

Becca twisted in her seat. "He let you look at it?"

Zach shook his head. "He left it where I could look while he went through Alex's old yearbooks so he could work on his best man's speech."

"Thin," Becca commented. "Did he say why?"

"He intimated they're stuck and he wondered if I knew anything. I told him," Zach said, with satisfaction, "that I'm retired."

"But he still came over." She'd not spent a lot of time with Logan Ferris, but she liked him. And she had a feeling there was another wedding in Zach's future. She wondered if it would help Zach to watch *Father of the Bride.*

The car stopped at a light and Zach gave her a grin that reminded her so much of the boy he'd been her heart stuttered. Like her younger self, the boy she'd crushed on was still in there. They'd grown up and lived through the same fifty years, separate but parallel in the time they'd passed through. It was a different kind of bond, but a bond just the same.

"He did." He accelerated again. "Barbara Betty is their top suspect, but I can tell Ferris doesn't like her for it."

"Anyone else on their list?" They'd have access to resources she and Zach didn't. She had a thought. "Was it poison, in the dinner?" Okay, that felt like a *Clue* question.

He must have thought it, too, because he chuckled. "Wasn't in his food, so must have been his glass. But nothing in his glass on the table."

"Whoever killed him must have swapped it or Georgy lost track of it and got another one," Becca mused. She'd gone through at least three cups that night. Had to keep putting them down for the hugs. "We mixed it up more than I thought we would during the mixer."

Zach grinned again. "No surprise that the witness statements are all over the place, but they were able to add a few names to the suspect list. Bubba was on the list until he fell off the ladder. Actually, he's still on the list, but toward the bottom."

That seemed like a metaphor somehow. "Sounds like a long list," Becca said.

"Well, Mary Magdalene was sitting next to Barbara Betty and Lisa Linda next to her. But witnesses placed Donna May, Daisy Dixie, Bettina Bailey, Mary Joanne Rivet, and your friend Dot talking to, or near Georgy during the mixer."

"A very long list," Becca said with a sigh. She frowned. "Why is Bubba the only guy on the list?"

"Frank Ray died and, well, poison is usually..." Zach trailed off, giving her a wary look.

"A woman's weapon." That's what all the mysteries she read claimed, too. It was a weapon that didn't require physical force. She had a thought. "What kind of poison was it?" If it was something exotic...

"Digitoxin."

"Oh." She was quiet for a couple of blocks. "Any of the suspects taking it?" Though the murderer could have used foxglove to make her own. "Or an avid gardener? Of course all they had to do was Google it," she finished with a sigh before he could answer.

"Which is why Ferris came to me."

Zach's satisfied tone came from satisfaction his son had failed, and not because the two of them might have a clue, Becca thought with an inward grin. Men. Good thing Alex hadn't asked for their help because right now, she couldn't see what they brought to the table.

"What did you tell Logan?" Becca asked, not completely innocently.

He picked up on it, shot her a look before he said, "I told him I'd think about it." He scowled. "If it was some old grudge, it's not obvious."

"I know who might know, but she's a suspect," Becca said.

"Who—" he stiffened. "Mary Magdalene."

"The class newsletter," Becca finished.

* * *

Zach did not know why they needed a rehearsal dinner. Who didn't know what to do at a wedding? Every time he turned around there was a new wedding show on television, or this or that character on a show tying the knot. At least all the kids were here, or they'd all been texting the missing siblings with the news about him and Becca.

That had been funny. The only face not surprised was Nell's. Even his girls had missed the signs.

He could still put one over on them. Not quite senile yet.

They'd all made friends with Becca during the wedding planning, so it would be hard for them to back off now. That was funny, too. Becca was in deep, too, he thought with satisfaction. He loved it when a plan came together. Though it wasn't locked down. Something was bothering Becca, and as soon as the wedding was over, he intended to ask her. Was gonna get it wrapped up and finalized before one of his kids played spoiler. Or one of hers.

So they'd all better get used to it, including Becca. She sat there visiting with Hannah, who still looked a bit shell-shocked. But it didn't take long for Becca's super power to take effect. Hannah began to relax—Zach saw a tiny smile twitching at the edges of Becca's mouth. For just an instant, her gaze flicked his way. Too quick for Hannah to notice, but Zach knew Becca had felt him watching her.

He grinned to himself. Oh yeah. He had it made.

"So, dad..." Ingrid's voice trailed off when he shifted to face her. An over bright smile curved her lips, but her eyes were a bit shocked, a bit worried. "You and...Becca?"

He waited, watched her until she shifted uneasily, then said, "It was sure nice of Sarah to host this do. We're a crowd without anyone else mixed in."

Ingrid's lips twitched, and her smile turned real. "Yeah, it's real nice of her."

Zach's gaze shifted to Nell's best friend. Sarah was a fine looking gal. Long and blonde. Reminded him a bit of Georgette. At least two of his sons showed signs of noticing, too. He'd be disappointed in them if they didn't. He half nodded toward the three of them.

"Anything there?"

Ingrid stared at him for a long moment, then she said, "So, how about them Saints?"

* * *

Becca drifted to the back of Sarah's dining room, then slipped into the hall. The old house was beautiful, a classic St. Charles Avenue mansion. Sarah had given her the tour when she'd picked Nell up here the first time. Nell, Becca had quickly learned, could drive but didn't like to. She biked or rode the streetcar.

Becca studied the long bench. It looked a tad more comfortable than the stairs, so she crossed to it and sank down. She slipped her shoes off—even the comfy ones got less so as the hours passed—and wiggled her toes. She rested her hands on material smoothed to a shine through long years. Despite the sense of it being old, Sarah had managed to make it feel welcoming. She glanced at the small table next to the bench and spotted Nell's sketchbook. She bit her lip.

It would be like looking in their medicine cabinet, so she looked away and saw Nell in the opening grinning at her.

"Go ahead. That's the one from the shower you asked about."

Becca laughed. "Should I be afraid?"

"Very."

Since life had delivered her harder challenges that seeing herself as a fruit or vegetable, Becca picked it up and flipped back the cover. Images spilled onto the page as if Nell had been in a rush to capture the figures before she lost them. Indeed, some of them did have a feeling of trying to run away, though they'd been "composed" into a fruit bowl on the page.

Nell's future sisters-in-law were easy to pick out. They were a bunch of bananas, clustered to one side. It took her a minute to find herself. "A pear?"

Nell sat down next to her, her finger tracing the shape. "You weren't that easy."

Becca opened her mouth to ask if it was her shape-lessness that made her hard, then decided she did not want to know. She moved to the other side of the "bowl."

"What kind of fruit is that?" It was round and had a spiky red surface.

"It's a rambutan. No one believes me, but I research fruit and vegetables all the time," Nell said, sounding just a bit miffed.

Becca chuckled, then felt herself stiffen as she processed the face integrated into the rambutan. Nell felt her stiffen, her gaze shifting from page to Becca.

"What's wrong?"

Becca knew her eyes had widened, her finger touching the face. "I think I know who did it. I just...why?"

Nell looked down and stiffened, too.

The face merged into the fruit had subtle hints of malice in the lines. How had Nell managed to make the eyes so cold?

"Sometimes I'm surprised by what my eyes see," Nell admitted. "Who—she's one of my gnarly relatives, isn't she?"

"And one of my gnarly classmates." Becca had sensed the connection, but this confirmed her instincts.

She stared at the face. "I know she did it, but we haven't a hope in Hades of proving it."

* * *

He and Becca were the first to leave the rehearsal dinner. Now it was just the wedding and the reception tomorrow. Maybe he shouldn't wait. Maybe he should just ask her, but women loved weddings. Made them all sentimental. He'd met Helen at a wedding. And Becca seemed a bit distant as they walked down the sometimes lit street. He'd had to park three blocks from Sarah's place. She had parking in the rear, but his kids had filled that up fast. Hadn't even apologized.

He glanced at Becca when they walked into a circle of light cast by a working street light.

"You okay? My kids didn't say anything?" Or do anything? He could still punish them if they had. Come to think of it, they should all still be grounded.

She gave a small start. "Sorry. No, they were fine. Better than I expected, actually."

"Then what's wrong?" Was she finally going to tell him what was holding her back? He might be a guy, but even he could tell that.

She slowed. "I know who killed Georgy."

"What?" He came to a dead stop and pulled her around to face him.

She frowned. "I just can't figure out why."

"Becca," Zach said, with controlled precision, "if you don't tell me a name, I might have to shake you."

"I can help you with that."

They both jerked and half turned toward the shadows on the non-street side of the rutted sidewalk.

"Bettina?" Becca said it in her super power calm voice.

"Bettina?" Zach's tone wasn't close to calm. More like shocked and stunned. He tried to think if he even knew what she looked like, back then or now. He knew her name from the police report, but he didn't remember her from the reunion. "That's who tried to run me down?"

Becca jerked, and he remembered he hadn't told her about that.

"Sorry," he muttered.

He heard a rustle and a hand holding a gun emerged from the deep shadows. Behind the gun, pale eyes gleamed.

"At least tell me why," he said, when it seemed the finger in the trigger guard began to tighten. There was a pause, and it seemed the hand relaxed some.

"Yes, please," Becca said, still in her calm voice.

He knew she was as tense as he was because she gripped his hand so hard his fingers were going a bit numb.

"They were too friendly," Bettina finally said, her voice half whine, half defensive.

They? So she had killed at least one more person than Georgy.

"Who was friendly?"

"It started with James John. On the Facebook. He flirted with you, Becca."

"James John...flirted with me on Facebook." Becca clung to him, trying to keep the shock out of her voice. "I don't remember."

"You didn't respond," Bettina sounded approving. "Not even when Larry Gary said he couldn't wait to see you again."

"Were...you worried about me, Bettina?"

Zach wished he dared look at Becca. He didn't dare take his eyes off the gun, even though he knew the odds of him getting to her in time were not great, even if she was as old they were. She twitched wrong—though her aim couldn't be great, could it? The gun wasn't wobbling at all though. That wasn't a good sign.

"It's been a long time since John died."

Her husband? Zach didn't think Becca's grip could get tighter, but he was wrong. It could. He didn't dare move, either.

"Yes, it has." A tense pause. "Did you...know John?"

"I worked with him the last year." Bettina's breathing turned rapid and shallow. "He was a good man."

"Yes, he was." Another pause. "I didn't know you knew him."

"I didn't know you were his wife until the funeral."

"Why didn't you...I don't remember you there." A different note crept into Becca's voice. She shifted, then stopped.

"I didn't say anything. John was gone and...you and I, we weren't friends."

"No." The word dropped into the space between the two women.

Bettina gave a kind of laugh. Like a sputter, but amused, too.

"You think we had an affair."

"Did you?"

Zach didn't know how she did it. The tone was even, though the super power was gone, turning her voice flat.

"I wish. I loved him. He was loyal. So loyal." A sigh in the shadows. "Such a good man."

Did she know she'd moved closer, more of her emerging from the shadows?

"You were a good wife." The gun shifted toward Zach. "Until now." Then it shifted in Becca's direction. "How can you betray his memory after so long? He deserved better."

Zach slowed his breathing, trying to keep his cool. He'd thought he was the target, but now he was pretty sure they both were. But surely someone driving by would notice? And his kids, they'd be heading home soon, wouldn't they? He and Becca were standing dead center of the street light.

Of course a wrong move...

He thought he heard a rustle off to the side and spoke quickly, "It has been a long time, Bettina. How long was Becca supposed to be faithful to a dead man?"

"Until she's dead, too." Her tone said that was obvious.

"John," Becca hesitated, as if choosing her words, "didn't want me to mourn him forever. He told me to find someone."

"But you didn't. Because you couldn't. No one is as good as John." The barrel turned in Becca's direction again. "You forgot, but I didn't. This is for John."

Zach could see her finger starting to tighten and pushed Becca to the side as a bright light flashed into Bettina's face. Her hand's jerked up to cover her face. The barrel flashed, and she fell backwards.

Figures, most likely some or all of his children, swarmed in from all directions. Zach moved to block Becca's view of the shattered face. His hands gripped her shoulders, and he tried to grin as adrenaline shuddered through him.

"Can't believe she tried this when the Bakers were gathered together." He felt her shudder and pulled her in close, despite the kids. It was noisy enough he could whisper in her ear, "I love you, Becca."

* * *

This time, Becca noticed with as much amusement as she could feel after almost getting shot, Alex had to listen to his dad. At some point, Nell and Sarah had joined the crowd. And a Lucky Dog truck. Didn't those guys ever sleep?

I love you, Becca.

And she loved him. The words would have come out

her mouth if there hadn't been a huge knot of fear and relief and remembering stuck in her throat. She hadn't been able to say anything. And a part of the past held her right now. The moment when she'd thought John and Bettina—her world had been rocked, even if it had rocked back.

They'd never know all the pieces of the Bettina puzzle, but it seemed obvious, she'd gained enough information to try to mess up Nell's wedding, though it wasn't clear what that had to do with Becca.

"I'll bet grandma dearest asked her to do it," Nell said. "Either she didn't know, or didn't care, she was launching crazy into everything."

Nell sounded resigned. It was hard to have any illusions left, Becca supposed, when the grandma dearest in question was in jail for trying to have her killed.

"It could have been any of them," Alex growled.

Nell had moved close to him. "Try not to think about it. They're going to be at the wedding tomorrow. It will just make it more awkward."

Becca heard a laugh come out her mouth, felt the relief of it as her body began to unlock.

Zach came over and leaned against the car next to her. Becca eased her hand into the crook of his crossed arms. He lowered them and took her hand, looking down at her.

"You okay?"

"I am." The words were husky, so she cleared her throat and tried again. "I am fine. And I love, you, too."

POSTLUDE

Becca stood next to Zach as his brother, Charlie, walked a radiant Nell down the aisle, her gaze fixed on Alex as she passed between family and Family, with her chin held high. Alex looked like he'd caught the moon and the sun, and possibly the stars.

Which was as it should be. They'd both won the only lottery that really mattered in Becca's opinion.

"Dearly beloved, we are gathered here today…"

It was a miracle they were gathered anywhere. It could have ended very differently if not for Zach and his Baker's Dozen.

Zach had had a firm grip on her hand since he helped her out of the car. There'd been an interesting spring in his walk and a look in his eyes that made her smile. She knew that look. It might be a throwback to a different time, but it was their time. She had no problem with him thinking, "I'm the *man*."

He'd faced down death and got the gal—the old gal—as his just reward. He hadn't asked her yet, but he was confident. He probably should be. Her issues hadn't melted away—she'd seen them in the mirror this morning—but death had a way of putting things in stark perspective.

She hadn't planned on falling in love again but then who did? Okay, Zach had probably planned it. It was cute and sweet and yes, a bit annoying he'd gotten his way, and now he thought he'd been both devious and clever, but she could live with that.

She could *live* with that.

"Do you take this woman..."

Becca glanced up at Zach. Found him looking at her. A question had pushed out the "I'm the man" look. A question filled with hope. His fingers tightened on hers when Alex said, "I do."

"Do you take this man..."

Her lips trembled a bit, and her saggy bits tried to tuck in. But despite it all, she smiled because she knew, and he knew, that somehow it was going to be okay. In fact, it might even be wonderful.

THANK you for reading *Louisiana Lagniappe!* I hope you enjoyed it. While you're waiting for the next book, I hope you'll check out some of my back list books. :-)

To find out about all my releases, be sure to sign up

for my New Release eZine and get a free eBook by visiting my website.

If you enjoyed this book, I hope you'll consider leaving a review. It's not just because I'm needy (even though I try not to be!). Reviews help other readers decide which books to buy. :-)

FROM DO WAH DIDDY DIE

For more New Orleans fun, try *Do Wah Diddy Die*:

Luci Seymour - sexy & free spirited - returns to steamy New Orleans in search of the father she's never met. She finds murder, mayhem, love and adventure when her timing puts her directly in the sights of an elderly hit couple and a con man's last scam.

Mickey Ross was not a happy man.

He'd just come off a two-day stakeout and had the rumpled suit and unshaven chin to prove it. He was tired. He was cranky. And he wasn't home in bed having that dream where the cover girl for Sports Illustrated was rubbing sun tan lotion onto his back.

He looked at where he didn't want to be, but the waiting area of the New Orleans International Airport didn't fade to something more pleasing. Nor did the stuffed pig dangling at the end of his arm vanish into the nightmare realm where it belonged.

Mickey glared down at it. Bad enough for a cop to be keeping company with any pig, but this pig, well, if it's lurid pink and purple surface was any indication, it had never been a beauty. Time had rubbed away the fluff from its surface and left one sorry black eye hanging by a single thread over the patchy remains of a black grin on its square snout. Its tattered ensemble began and ended with a limp ribbon knotted around a fat neck.

In an effort to distance himself from his ratty companion, Mickey held it by the tatty end of the ribbon and twirled it with more than a hint of vindictiveness.

In between twirls, he pondered the unkind fate that had landed him in this fix. If Eddie hadn't decided to end sixty years of bachelorhood, he wouldn't be waiting for a damn flower girl for the damn wedding, with only a stuffed pig for an introduction. Who flew in a little girl for a geriatric wedding anyway? New Orleans was full of little girls who'd probably love tossing petals. But no, they had to import one, then pick a total stranger to collect her—with an obnoxious pig as the icebreaker. Convenient that Eddie had discovered pressing business in Mandeville tonight.

The least he could have done was warn him about the old ladies. How could his own uncle send him into battle, into that minefield of weirdness, without even a warning? A minefield that had kept going off in his face no matter what he did, a horror—except for the one small oasis of sanity known as Miss Gracie, who had saved him from the stuffed dragon, but not the pig.

He just wished he knew where Eddie's Unabelle—was that a name to make a guy flinch—fit in with the Seymour's. She didn't seem to be a relative. She was just...there, like a black hole. He sure hoped the lights were on in her upper story for Eddie or he'd learn there were worse things than a lonely retirement.

A stir at the gate quickly became arrival as passengers filtered off the plane. With the end in sight, Mickey straightened in hope.

That's when it occurred to his weary brain that a stuffed pig might be a less than adequate introduction to the kid. What had possessed the parents to entrust their kid to the uncertain care of three batty old ladies? He studied each small, whining arrival, wondering which one was his. A security guard loomed up on one side and he had to produce his badge.

The case against Eddie just kept building.

A woman emerged from the breezeway and paused to get her bearings. Mickey straightened in an utter and complete moment-of-silence respect for the best legs he'd ever been privileged to lay eyes upon. The cop part of him was vaguely aware she was in her late twenties, maybe early thirties, almost of a height with him and the possessor of a slender build. Her hair was dark and cut short around a face made interesting by its square jaw and straight, dark brows. Mouth was nice, too. Full and lush and lined in red.

He left off admiring her legs to contemplate her mouth, but his attention was drawn lower again when the legs went into motion. Brief appearances by her thighs, between the slash of her dark skirt, had him tugging at a too-tight tie. It took him a few seconds to realize that she'd stopped right in front of him.

With extreme reluctance, he dragged his gaze back to eye level. Her head was angled, her gaze directed toward the pig with a seriousness it didn't deserve. Just for a moment, something in the angle of her jaw had him wondering if he'd met her, but he dismissed the notion. A guy couldn't forget those legs.

His gaze drifted down again, but he flashed back to attention when she stepped closer, her nose bare inches from his, her lashes lifting with lust-building slowness to reveal emerald green depths.

His tie tightened to near strangulation level, but he couldn't move, let alone do something about it. Green eyes were always trouble for him. Too bad proximity and hormones took the edge off caution. If his partner, Delaney, were here, he'd recognize the signs of Mickey on the verge of falling in lust again. But Delaney wasn't here. The lucky bastard was in bed.

Carpe Diem. Mickey knew his smile was his best

opening gambit and produced it with practiced ease. "Hello."

Luci studied the smile, recognized the confidence and the intent behind it. She'd met smiles like this one. Smiles that were confident of their charm. Smiles that expected weak knees and a cessation of rational thought. It was fortunate she had a built-in immune system to charming smiles and didn't ever do rational thought. It went with being a Seymour, though her knees, just for a moment, signaled a willingness to depart from the norm. She reminded herself she was the result of a departure from the norm and said, "That's my pig."

"When it comes to creating stories with offbeat humor and outrageous situations, Pauline Baird Jones is in a class by herself. A most excellent experience!" *RT Book Reviews*

To buy this book, click here.

FROM OPEN WITH CARE

Christmas has never been so....green...

———————

The drive to crazy town was a good distraction from the Thing that Virginia Prescott did not want to think about. It helped that she needed to focus on the snowy, winding road in steadily worsening weather.

And if that didn't keep her mind off the Thing, there were her passengers.

It was probably her imagination that inimical gazes bored holes into her back. Gini risked a look in the rear view mirror and caught Isaac looking at her. He met her gaze for a second that felt longer than that, then it slid away with more composure than Gini had had at nine. Her twin sister's new stepson was a little scary.

Gini was still trying to figure out how Isaac and his

sister had landed in the rear seat of her rented SUV. There were unmistakable signs they were not willing passengers for this trip. Isaac wasn't openly hostile—yet —but Daphne had made it clear Gini would have to bust an impossible move to rise to the level of pond scum.

Gini didn't blame them. They'd had no say in the very recent marriage of their dad, and it was clear that their absent-minded-professor-ish parent had either forgotten to brief them, or punted that job to her. Bif and Vanessa both worked at NASA, in the same department. It was how they met. But Gini didn't entirely buy into the "emergency" that had left her holding the kids. Not that she begrudged the newlyweds some alone time, but they'd better show up for Christmas. Or sooner. Both of them. Period.

The snow was showing up. From what she could see in the headlights, it was going to be a very white Christmas. It occasionally snowed in Dallas, but for the whitest of white holidays, she'd always had to come home. The swirling flakes had looked pretty dancing around the deer antler arch at the edge of the small Wyoming town where she and Van had grown up. The sight of it stirred her happy memory cortex. Would Van make it in time to watch *White Christmas* with them? Even if they didn't sing the "Sisters" song out loud—which would probably be an even worse sin than Van marrying the kids' dad— they'd exchange a look that said they were singing inside their heads. It was their song. And in the morning, after the presents and the feast—which could be great or awful depending how much access mom gave them to the kitchen this year—there'd be deep, white drifts for snowball fights and snow angels and sledding and getting so cold hot chocolate was necessary for survival—

As if Daphne sensed her happy thoughts and deplored them, Gini heard a sigh—and possibly felt it ruffle her hair—from the teen's side of the vehicle. It had a glare attached that drilled her between the shoulder blades. Sucked to be thirteen. And the two kids lived with their mom, so their dad not showing up at the airport to collect them would have upped the disappointment factor by an equation only Van was smart enough to figure out.

Gini had tried to lighten the atmosphere with some carols—the only music the radio could pick up—but that just seemed to expand the cloud of 'not happy' to the point of stifling, despite the headphones firmly clamped over Daphne's ears. She couldn't remember exactly how it felt to be thirteen, but she did remember not liking much, including herself. In distant memory of that awful time, Gini turned the happy—and the music—off. It was the least she could do. Possibly the only thing she could do.

Isaac also wore headphones. His game gave off an eerie green glow, like they were in a war bunker or something.

Ho, ho, ho.

She was kind of surprised that Grif hadn't responded to her text that she'd collected his children from the Cody airport. She'd even left off the guilt attachment, which was hugely magnanimous of her in her opinion. It was possible her timing was awkward. Or maybe there really was an emergency, though she couldn't imagine what emergency NASA could have. Daphne for sure hadn't believed it, if her extreme eye roll was any indication. Discontent was an almost visible haze back there, though it did go with the green glow.

She saw a familiar half rock, half log gate and took the turn. Almost there now. She kinda felt like she ought to warn them that there might be worse than an unwanted step aunt to face at the cabin, but she didn't know what version of crazy she'd find. Her mom, who had given birth very late in life, had been a solid twelve on a ten point weird scale—with ten being the most extreme—even before age had started to degrade her synapses. At least the incoming quirky-to-bat-crap-crazy-weird was a great distraction from—but she wasn't thinking about the Thing.

Her SUV swept around a corner and the edge of the lights caught a blur of movement. Gini didn't hit the brakes, but she did take her foot off the gas. The thickening swirl of flakes remained mercifully clear of solid objects. She did not need to slam her rental into a deer. Not that—but the light and night must be playing tricks on her. She thought she'd seen a glimpse of a green little —but that was crazy, even for crazy town.

She'd checked the weather about a hundred times before boarding her plane, but the storm had stubbornly refused to commit until she was on the ground and headed for the cabin—a cabin her mom should *so* not be occupying, with or without a live-in care giver. And yet here Gini was, ferrying the reluctant step-grand kids over the frozen crick and through the snowy woods to step-grandma's house. She just prayed that Van and Grif would make it before the storm closed the road.

The eerie glow on Isaac's side of the car faded to black. For no reason she could identify, that made her uneasy.

———

If you like offbeat humor and outrageous situations, you'll love *Open With Care*!

ALSO BY PAULINE BAIRD JONES

Available in print, digital and audio.

Romantic Suspense

The Big Uneasy Series:

Relatively Risky (1)

Family Treed (A Big Uneasy Short Story)

Dead Spaces (2.0)

Louisiana Lagniappe (3.0)

Worry Beads (4.0)

Fais Do Do Die (5.0)

The Big Uneasy Bundle

Lonesome Lawmen Series:

The Last Enemy

Byte Me

Missing You

Lonesome Mama (Bonus short story)

(The *Lonesome Lawmen* is also available as a digital bundle)

Do Wah Diddy Die

The Spy Who Kissed Me

Perilously Fun Fiction Bundle (includes *The Spy Who Kissed Me* and *Do Wah Diddy Die*. Bonus: *Do Wah Diddy Delete Short Story Collection*)

Dangerous Dance

Dangerous Duet - 2020

Science Fiction Romance/Paranormal

Project Universe Series:

The Key (book 1)

Girl Gone Nova (book 2)

Tangled in Time (book 3)

Steamrolled (book 4)

Kicking Ashe (book 5)

Found Girl (book 6)

Lost Valyr (book 7)

Maestra Rising (book 8)

Project Enterprise: The Short Stories

Time Trap: A Project Enterprise Series Short Story

The Real Dragon

Operation Ark: A Project Enterprise Story

Nebula Nine (time travel adventure)

Open With Care (Christmas collection that includes, "Riding For Christmas" and "Up on the House Top"

Specters in the Storm: A paranormal/steampunk/science fiction romance novella

Out of Time (World War II Time Travel Romance)

Just in Time (An Out of Time Adventure)

An Uneasy Future

(A science fiction romance mystery series set in future New Orleans)

Core Punch (1.0)

Sucker Punch (2.0)

One Two Punch: An Uneasy Future Bundle

Short Story Collections

Project Enterprise: The Short Stories

Do Wah Diddy Delete

Let's Fall in Love

The Real Dragon and other short stories

ABOUT THE AUTHOR

Award-winning, *USA Today* Bestselling author Pauline never liked reality, so she writes books. She likes to wander among the genres, rampaging like Godzilla, because she does love peril mixed in her romance.

To find out more about Pauline or her books:
http://paulinebjones.com
pauline@paulinebjones.com